Composed

Jack Babcock

Pistol River Press
2021

Composed

Heidi Barth thought up the title

it was going to be Strength but Ken
didn't like it.

Heidi takes care of a bower at Providence
day center. flowers plants. it's a sweet place
to visit. I am composed. this book is dedicated
to her and to Joe who fixed my wheelchair.

my last book was called Comma Coma
Comma.

how apt to follow it with Composed.

great poetry----- the gift of
precision
in ecstasy

Edith Wharton

Table of Contents

Here Comes Everybody

is a character
in James Joyce's
final book Finnegan's Wake

HCE

was Joyce saying finally at last
that he liked everyone
at least found
everyone interesting.

he loves everyone

Finnegan's wake is in a sense
an optimistic book

everyone is the hero

everything is beautiful

yet Joyce the younger wrote

history is a nightmare from
which I'm trying to recover

but that is the past

HCE looks to the future.

Vault

Bob Dylan said it best
I mean no harm nor put fault
on anyone who lives in a vault

that has been my life
retreating from painful reality.
escaping at times like
Mr. Tambourine man.

oddly maybe not oddly
John Donne wrote

churches are best for prayer
that have least light
to see god only I go out of sight
and to 'scape stormy days
I choose an everlasting night.

well it seems like the same sentiment.

must we avoid reality?

face it like a man say some
are you a coward said my friend John K

well I dodged the draft.

I'm a peacenik. a pacifist.

but I put my money where my mouth is

I donated blood regularly for years.

6 gallons in all

that was not cowardly.

authors note:

my brother said I didn't dodge the
draft. I merely flunked the physical
because of schizophrenia.

he was a captain in the air force.

Train

it'd be great
to have to catch a train

early one morning
and to escape this life these cares

a train to a new country
an escape.

Baseball

illness

I have 3 illnesses

schizophrenia
diabetes

and worst of all

acute kidney disease

3 strikes 3 strikes and you're out

 but I feel pretty well

Madness

I'm schizophrenic
I have no peace
upon these pages
I bleed! I weep!

and finally fatally
I pray for my decease.

Goddammit

I'm fucked up
I'm an ex-alcoholic
I hallucinate

poems are pretty things
at times
but can be
harsh and
ridiculous

I have
writ my poem
time to die
Goddammit.

2.
    Goddammit
poems are
fuckin ridiculous things

oh god
hell.

Alcoholism

14 years of sobriety

is that wise?

I miss the conviviality
Mr. Tambourine man

but

1. pain in my side
that occurs when drinking
has gone away.

2. I take meds

3. voices:

mentally ill
alcoholic

4. less paranoid sober
   no dui

friends say drink up

guy in AA said get new friends

I did.........!

Memoir

my books are memoirs

1. my battle with schizophrenia
2. a schizophrenics look at beauty
3. poetry and literary criticism.

people say my writing is raw, dark
and depressing. i think its light often

Dickens

I made it through David Copperfield
on the kindle. I didn't like it
a lot. Dickens wrote that it was
his favorite book.

I found it wordy contrived needlessly
complex but the characters are well drawn.

I remember liking Great Expectations in high school.

and I loved a Christmas Carol.

our sixth-grade teacher read us A Tale
of Two Cities pretty scary for young
folk.

Dickens is great but I don't think
David Copperfield is his best book.

Witches Brew

with what pleasure
I first read about
the witches in Macbeth
or the ghost in Hamlet
or for that matter the
spirits in Dickens' tale
A Christmas Carol

Shakespeare and Dickens
appeal to the kid in us
by using the supernatural
to tell their tales.

are the witches real?
is the ghost real?
are the spirits real?

it's a moot point.
they serve their purpose

and we have the fabulous stories.

    Q.E.D.

Mist

Stephen king's story the mist
is pretty scary.
not as scary as Poe's tales tho.
not as scary as the cask of amontillado.
nowhere near as horrifying as the pit
and the pendulum. not as intriguing
as murders in the rue morgue.

But the idea of a mist that covers
groups of people is quite clever
and mysterious.

the writing is a little awkward.
Poe is the better writer.

King is popular tho. I haven't
given up on him.

I feel like I'm in a mist
trying to find the meaning.

Gaylord Kinnell

I'll have to google Gaylord Kinnell
I like his poem Blackberry Eating
but I wonder about the author

has he written other simple poems
about nature?

My poems are about art

what is it?

how is it?

why is it?

Writer

I collect words

a writer

Joyce was the ultimate
wordsmith

breaking words down
and reassembling them

Shakespeare used words

to the greatest advantage

man's loveliest invention language

Tragedy

I write poems
down
in pen and paper

but
what's the point
I can't read my writing

and poems
are gone
forever

some were lousy
but that doesn't help
cuz some were good
and I feel
the tragedy

but I have
this poem
anyway.

Muse

time to write a poem

the muse is gone

or broken

but its important

to try

so I pen

I get books from the library by mail

I love to read

but I have the kindle too

I got complete works of Shakespeare

for 49 cents
hard to beat

I read quickly with the kindle

but I love a book

I will do both!

Grammar

affect   verb
effect   noun

imminent
eminent

words

assiduous
tautology
garrulous
ascetic
protagonist
sycophant
timorous
harbinger
temerity
supercilious
asymptomatic
avatar
juggernaut
factious
untoward

Words

fun

what a word

though

what a word

abstemious

yes

what a word!

Quilt

my mother's afghan
lies quietly on my bed

should I craft a poem
like making an afghan

I can picture mom
working quietly
on the quilt

a stillness
the quiet of her fingers
working away

yet there's a product

should I craft a poem
instead of writing one

if I get a product. yes.

this poem is done. finis. love jack

Ring-a-ding

the topless dancer looked at my hand
at my ring and said that looks pretty
on you.

I had said to her that her garb looked
pretty on her.

my typing manual said to use that
construction instead of you look pretty
in that.

it was an amethyst ring, a family heirloom.
it was beautiful.

later it was lost or more likely stolen.
I'd had a couple robberies and had also
let some riff-raff into my house on occasion.
just wanted to use that word riff-raff.

the good news was that I found another ring
in a family jewel box. it was beautiful.
gold-plated.

when I was visiting Emmett and Fran's, he
remarked on my ring. I said it was
fool's gold. he scraped it with some tool
and told me it was real gold.

in big letters raised on the ring were
the letters MG.

I had made a genealogy chart showing

the Babcock family history. and there
on the chart was Mary Elizabeth Goodlive
who married T.J. McCarver circa 1850.

rings are mystical, mysterious important.
.
I gave my niece aunt Liz's rings. beautiful
small and subtle. her name is Mary Elizabeth
Babcock.
she loved the rings.

when dad passed I gave his ring to my cousin William
McCarver beers. it is so cool. a moonstone.
doesn't suit me but it was perfect for bill.
wear it well bill.

and......

i got a spoon ring at the saturday market
in Eugene. cool.

rings are mystical mysterious important

Little Town

every Wednesday I visit
a little town called
therapy, New York.

it isn't new York really.
but it is a little town.

I see a therapist Margaret.
it's a zoom conference.
I need help.

I'm a schizophrenic.
I used to hear voices.
perilous horrible voices.
some good ones too.

Margaret helps me see the world
in a less stark way. she smooths
out the wrinkles.

yes

I'm not a thief
or a hitman
or even a liar.

well 2 out of 3.

I don't drink
I don't smoke
I don't blow dope

or use cain

a voice says
to do these things

help Margaret

    ****

Margaret suggested
I listen to music.

I told her I lost
my Dylan Christmas cd
which is a lot better
than it sounds.

so I put on a
Janis Joplin cd

odd is that I heard
a voice to

talk to bob Dylan

and that

I am Janis Joplin

    ****

well

I push on.

Skateboard

we were in high school, Wayne and I
we were friends, which meant that
he rode aloft my shoulders smarted.

But he was fun too. We both had skateboards.
Wayne's board was big and beautiful with
inlaid wood. Mine purchased at Fred Meyer
was small white and nifty.

We boarded Walters Lane and the west hills
cemetery. But my happiest hours were spent
on my board in our basement.

After school I would hop on my board and
go round and round the basement. Upstairs
mom was making brownies, resting whatever.

At night I would drink tea and do my studies.
Geometry, English, business law.

I did well in school. Skateboarding was just the
right amount of exercise.

I took my board to college but put it
in a free box. I've often regretted that
for it was my life in high school.

Aquarium

I was crying. my tropical fish
had all died. I was in the fifth grade.
I bought the fish at the department store
Meier and Frank.

I rushed home put them in the tank
and half an hour later they were all
belly-up.

Mother put her arm around me. kind mother.

no one told me I had to take the chlorine
out of the water supply

my tank was in my room in the basement.

at night the hum of the air supply motor
would help me go to sleep. the soft lighting
in the tank helped too. the light shone
through the plentiful plant life ferns moss etc.
I liked the plants as much as the fish.

finally I got fish after taking out the chlorine
with drops of some chemical: neon tetra black tetra
glow lite tetra aeneas catfish angelfish swordtail
and not least of all guppies.
the fish swam through the lighted plant life. i had
planted the tank with care.

it was relaxing to watch the fish look at the plant life
listen to the motor and hear the bubbling of the air
supply.

I loved my tank.

On Writing

people say my writing
is raw dark and depressing.
I try to write
so that I will be understood.
it is fairly simple writing.
I try to avoid wordiness.
as to the adjective when in doubt
strike it out. and I try to avoid
construction like very unique.
my writing is therapeutic.
I'm trying to recover from mental illness
schizophrenia.
that can be construed as raw and dark I guess.
I go on, wish me luck.

Clouds

looking at clouds today
they come tumbling down

cirrus cumulus

puffy and proud
they come tumbling down

the clouds

Lion

the lion
without the door
gets loose
makes a roar

trembling
frightened
no place
to bury my head

despite
all the books
I have read.

Mystery

one of my plants
a mystery pansy

looks like its thriving
the fern Gloria gave me
looks like its dying

I don't keep fish
they died too

i don't have a green thumb

but I've learned to love
every thing and every one

Dostoevsky said.

maybe I'm a bum

I've learned to love
everything and everyone.

Q.E.D.

Eyes

oh miserable I am Mithridates

I live with hope
yet I tell telling lies
my life is over
I'm afraid
I despair

there is no hope

for blasted eyes.

The Bird

the birds
wings cut the sky
another bird proud
has his own
way to fly
cutting the sky
hovering over his nest
as if to say
I am the best
his wings cut the sky
amazing you and I.

Desk

a yellow rose
seeks me out

my desk turns into
a large yellow rose

I need to write poems
so this one just popped up
beneath my desk

a large yellow rose

my desk was old anyway.

Time

it's 4:18 in the morn
four eighteen
time to write a poem
or watch twilight zone

make a drawing
write an essay

essay
drawing

four eighteen
in the morning.

Blue

I woke and donned

a blue shirt
a blue scarf
blue gloves

all in blue

went my love riding

on the bus to the nurses station

nurses were sweet

Candy was one

and Connie and Anna

and Stephanie and Natalie

and doctor Hotelling

and all in blue

went my love writing

a poem for the day

a visit to the clinic

yay!

Tide

first the tide rolls in
raising a stick a stone

an imagist poem

I can see the tide furling
is that a word?

throwing the stones
the gravel
up to the shore

receding

taking pages of poems

images

the sea
the surf
the stones

imagist poems

Impressionist Haiku

#1

Haiku
I can't master
oversleep

#2

the phone
keeps saying
low battery

#3

symphony in blue
is there a god?
I don't know

Joycean

#4

Bucks name for Stephen
Kinch the knife blade
how apropos

#5

a racehorse named

Buck mulligan
somebody bet on the bay

#6

I'm a failure with women
need a
Molly Bloom

#7

Hemingway
and black despair
Life is a meaningless hell

#8

Portland
April showers bring
may showers

#9

noses
lie cheat steal
I think I die

Thursday

vision of an empty classroom
chairs without coats on them

an economics professor
or
a sixth-grade teacher

just an empty chair
on a Thursday afternoon
in the summer.

Sunday

I had to do dialysis Saturday
I was frenzied Friday
and frantic Monday
but I woke to lovely Sunday

read a poem
recite a poem
get some z's
look at flowers
Heidi's bower

watch the waves
crawl up on the shore

yes its lovely Sunday.

Escorts

Allison and Gigi

early in the morn
at the doctor's office

Allison and Gigi
are the escorts

helping me undress
show my wound
to the doctor

Gigi speaks Russian
today it is English

they are so much help

thanks

jak aka Jack

Fred

I'm always surprised that

Fred is so even-tempered
and so good to me

it comes with being a carpenter I guess

Fred is a kind of Jesus

without the sloppy trappings.

he's made me picture frames

a chessboard and a clock etc.

...but most of all

he's a friend.

Barry

writing prompt

great minds

Barry reads Karl Marx

and understands it.
I don't

enuf said

he was fun too

great sense of humor

he had a big imposing library
I'd like to show him Powell's books

but he is nowhere to be found.

Jakee

one of my quadmates passed the other day.

I think she died from sadness.

she was always crying and screaming

didn't like to read or socialize much.
.
it made me sad

I wrote in my journal once:

get that girl some meds or therapy

or a dog or something.

I endured my illness with meds therapy

and a dog.

there but for the grace of god go I.

sound and fury

Joe

Biden won
I voted for him
I didn't celebrate

but I was relieved
life will be better for sure

but lots better?
I don't know

but I do know
that if trump had won

I'd continue to be
stoic cynical bitter
and sarcastic

but Biden won
and I can be
a loving human being

well that's a pipe dream
but maybe I can be myself.

a new cap with letters

   MGTF

  my god! the future!

Dad

happy father's day dad
tho you never celebrated it

have a happy day

play some crib

drink some early times

smoke

argue politics

but most of all
have a happy day dad!

Trump

my caregiver and 2 of my cousins
are voting for Trump

my friends hate him

I'll vote for Biden

why do people like Trump?

I posited 3 possibilities

1.foeign policy   e.g. China Israel

2. economy evinced by stock market

and most of all

3. laws and order

the downside

white supremacist

bib

brash ignorant bastard

so -

Portland

do I like Portland?
its where I live
for god's sake.

where I was born.

I like the flowering cherry trees.
I like Mr. Portland Ken Boddie.

I like the Jackson tower
my mom always called me Jackson.

Joyce wrote about Dublin
I write about Portland.

Portland has 20 parks
and the rose test gardens.

the zoo museums sports pavilion.
cool monuments like the elk.

lots of trees lots of bridges

Portland, my kind of town.

Rose City

I wrote an ode to Portland
how much I like the parks the library
the trees the bridges the rose gardens etc.

but there's a dark side to Portland too.

in my mind anyway.

it is not Starkfield as in Edith Wharton's novel
Ethan frome, but its close

to wit

the psychiatrist told me that I was seeing
reality too starkly.

stark

my landlady's name was Faye Starkey.

my boyhood friend was John Stark.

and to top it all off a main street
in Portland is Stark street.

in another life I would have left Portland

but this is my home, this is where I live.

it's a nice place.........

Mr. Portland

42

mister Portland
sweet as a rose
honoring our citizens
honoring our forest
honoring our gardens
honoring our monuments

reading the news

sweet as a rose
mister Portland

Ken Boddie

thanks Ken

Jack Babcock

Seaside

on tv they show Portland
the Fremont bridge
so exciting and alive

they also show Seaside, the head
and therefore the cove unseen

the head looks like a catfish
splayed out on the sand

but
I remember the cove
and

the gay downtown
with shops
Phillips candy
the arcade
the bakery
aromas abound

Seaside, my kind of town.

Bullshit Cowboy

everywhere you go
there are bullshit
cowboys. Mom used to call them boyos.
Guys who use women, who are
cavalier with the opposite sex.
Those who denigrate, disparage
ride aloft. Who brag about their
sexual conquests when they're actually
merely rude.

i won't name names but they are ubiquitous.

Bitches

the other side of the coin are bitches.

Molly Bloom said it best:

what a dreadful lot of bitches we are.

I like bitches tho. they're sexy
for one thing

Worm

a la Blake

the worm turns

us in distress!

the worm has found us out

we cannot bless

the cruel worm

us in distress

let the robin come

take him away

snatch him up!

Horse

I took him apples for lunch
and he crunched and crunched

a peaceful guy
the children liked him

prize winning barrel
racing champion

my guy Chuck

Riot

I'm upset about the rioters
in Portland. what are they doing to
our beautiful city?

I think of Yeats' poem the second coming
and the line 'the best lack all conviction
while the worst are full of passionate
intensity'.

the good news is my ring now fits on my
finger. I've lost weight I guess.

Difficult is the kindle. what do I read?
For now it is chamber music, poems by
James Joyce.

great but I need more.

Joyce I've read. Shakespeare? Dostoevsky
is difficult. dickens? David Copperfield
was long.

that leaves science fiction.

any suggestions friends?

Irish Song

here we go walking
singing and talking

here we go walking
down to Kildare

old woman old woman old woman
says I

where are you going
with broom so high

to sweep the cobwebs
off the sky

and I'll be back
tomorrow by and by

Fruitcake

I'm getting Tsega
a fruitcake for xmas

funny how many people
hate fruitcake

I like it a lot

a little fruitcake
and a cup of tea. yum

Suicide

my girlfriends were
always trying to ditch
themselves

do I lack charm

I mean them no harm

maybe I should ditch myself

I go on
there's more to this yarn

I love life. finis. jak

My Thoughts About Suicide

Sylvia Plath
Ann Sexton
Diane Arbus
Charlotte Gilman

a voice said

panic attacks
suicide attempts

when are we going to end all this

Charly committed suicide
and I probably will too

Dad used to say 'I want out'

a voice said

bleed to death
starve to death
freeze to death
choke to death

ah me!

Blessed

I was having a sad morning
I was in distress

so I called Val
and I was blessed

her sweet voice
was like honey to a bear

I was cheered!
and got some rest.

      thanks Val

      love Jack

Hope

a thing with feathers
you cannot tell why

go left go right
upside down

good and evil
is what I found!

Hamster

have you ever
begged a hamster for help

well I have

help Herms
help Herms
he passed

and Dante
came on the scene

it was not hell
but bliss

and Dante passed

hamsters live only
3 or 4 years.

Gratitude #1

John McEnroe
the tennis player
liked to thank his
parents for having him

thanks mom thanks dad

sometimes I think
I'm a mistake tho
an erratum

I have a brain disorder
schizophrenia

this isn't a poem

I can't write a poem
about gratitude

cept to say

thanks for the therapy

Margaret   love Jack

Gratitude # 2

Tsega, Saba, Nardaus, Erzana
help me in so many ways

Saba found my lost Bob Dylan
Christmas cd this morn.

I won't be alone at Christmas
while Dylan cranks out his tunes.

thanks Saba thanx Bob Dylan
and thanks Mollie for the cd.

Gratitude # 3

a poem for Tsega
I write one every day
in a way
she is sweet and kind
and doesn't mind
my many faults
the meals are good
and I am healthy.
thanks Tsega Kassa

Forecast

a little rain and cold
and if I may be so bold

cloud cover and drizzle

shades of the moon

a red moon
a harvest moon
a heather moon

the moons a balloon maybe

high surf
advisory for the coast

snow and cold
up in the mountains

and in the fountain------

A la Blake

the earthworm
helps in the garden
Let us bless!

the robin builds his nest
the robin kneels in the garden
tugs the worm.

let us bless.

My Paint Set

(my art box)

and my chess set
are virgins

they haven't been used

it's a little excitement
a little fun
a lot

the chess set
needs an opponent

the art set
needs some inspiration
some perspiration

I can do art by myself
chess takes two to tango

I'm like a kid at Christmas

the art box
has pencils crayons paints
and more

the chess set has
castles and kings
knights and queens
and more

if I'm an artist

am I also a chessist not
I'm a player

gawd I need an opponent

This poem it is done

well I can write
anyway.

Sex

the bee loses his stinger
and dies
the man loses hid stinger
and what

loses interest in sex?

buzz bump
buzz bump

buzz #?!#?

sex is overrated I hope

Poetry Is a Game

these poets play
a rigorous game of chess

obscure exotic chess

I make a few moves

some distress

do I play a poor game

yes exotic chess

do I know the rules?

when to rhyme
when to meter

it is sublime
this game of chess

imagist poets
romantic poets

or just damn poets

yes I can play

I'm a poet's poet

and it's a great game.

CNN

CNN is my default station. When

I don't know what to watch I watch

CNN. it's pretty good I think. I

like the people: Fareed Zakaria,

Victor-----. and Anderson Cooper.

People hate fox news. I don't.

They cover the news well and they

don't duck controversy.

Their politics......well....stink.

I don't like Sean Hannity, Tucker Carlson

or the five. CNN is my default station.

Bed

1.

I saw on the tube
an ad for a bed
king sized

in single bed Jack

it would be nice to do things in two

2.

doing things in one tho is nice
no petty quarrels
no intrigue no spice

one is just fine for now
two is too many maybe

my uncle used to say
that he was a lone angel

so be it. I'm an angel.   jak

Living

what's the point of living

if you can't

smoke a cigarette

drink a beer

blow some dope

or

drop some acid

what's the point

authors note:

14 years of sobriety

Love Matters

a child's poem
not a heavy tome
brings love and laughter
and what comes after
sweet words
and love that matters

Poems

my dog-eared pages
with my poems
lying by my obscure tomes

oh isn't life absurd!
well poetry is!

of this I am assured.

Calendar

a la Emily

Life is horrendous

Tuesdays are mournings

Wednesday don't mention it
I have no spirit

Thursday go back to Tuesday

Friday is a light day

the rest of the days
lie screaming in front of me.

p.s.

Saturday is a mystery

Sunday Monday
let's flee

Tuesday go back to--------

finis

Crying

I shall weep no more forever

who said?

Shakespeare?

who?

well it doesn't apply to me

it could tho

but I've seen some sad things

Joyce makes me cry too
even the Wake

his take on war and peace

so be it!

Fire

the red sun
peers thru the smoke
the news is near doom
I haven't had asparagus in years
or a banana split
the jazz pianist plays a riff
the president waves a flag
I hope for one last good meal
Red alert level 3.

Poetry

poems are precious things

today in writing group
we read
Miniver Cheevy
by E. A. Robinson
a masterpiece

he wanted to live
in a romantic world

but ended up
an alcoholic
in this world.

Democrats

Us Democrats
want to make
a better society

take a lot of heat
from the right wing

but this bird
needs 2 wings to fly

I'm left wing
and proud.

Therapy

I collect stamps for therapy
I see the world as sad and ugly
and stamp collecting brings
beauty and order to my world.

yes when I'm sad I peruse
my stamp collection. I visit
foreign lands or get an
American history lesson.

finis